STO

LO   R   '67

ALLEN COUNTY PUBLIC LIBRARY

ACPL ITEM

3 1833 04393 3826

DISCARDED

The Gypsy Tree

THE GYPSY TREE

By Ethel Collier

WITH ILLUSTRATIONS BY
Lajos Szalay

NEW YORK:
William R. Scott, Inc.

Library of Congress Catalog Card No. 64-13588
TEXT © 1966 BY ETHEL COLLIER. ILLUSTRATIONS © 1966 BY LAJOS SZALAY.
All Rights Reserved. Printed in U. S. A.

Contents

CO. SCHOOLS
C629057

1. A Chancy Thing

After Dirk glimpsed the white brick farmhouse down the road, his eyes wouldn't let go. "Let that be the house, let that be the house," he wished half aloud as they approached in the car.

"You said you never crossed your fingers for luck any more," Marni said, spying on him. She sat much lower in the back seat than he, and hadn't the view ahead.

He folded his arms, striving for a lordly look while taking care to cover his hands. Maybe luck charms weren't as important as they used to be. Still, when finding a new house was touch and go, what was the harm? "I can cross my fingers, can't I? It doesn't mean I have to believe," he said, having it both ways.

For a half-hour they had been just driving around the unfamiliar little city, from the outskirts in. First, they had passed the new research center where Mr. Jarus would work now, then massed roofs of houses lately built to climb a slope, and still on the outskirts, acres of sleek ground landscaped for light industry.

They passed an old section dipping to a small river. Stone piles, tracks and a freight station nudged sour-faced houses here. Children played in the dust, and as the car climbed a hill, Dirk looked back, vaguely troubled. But now the car came to a main street that smelled wonderfully of popcorn and yard goods. A turn, a climb again, and they skimmed past turn-of-the-century houses with porch-y fronts, broad-lapped and unstylish, and looking entirely pleased about it.

Now, well to the north of town, buildings thinned out. A lane dreamed off into a clump of trees, and the white brick farmhouse sat just ahead. Mr. Jarus slowed and turned in.

From the driveway, a little informal gravel sputtered up. The gravel petered out into wheel ruts and tufts of grass heading toward a wagonshed, a clear ancestor of garages. "Hey-y," said Dirk.

8

Then everyone was out of the car. Marni did a little jump and said in a rush of feeling, "MaywehaveitDaddymayyyywe?"

In the peculiar language that houses have, the old farmhouse spoke to Dirk and Marni. Mrs. Jarus went straight to a crumbling doorjamb. "That could be replaced," said Mr. Jarus. She made a joyless survey of the unpruned growth around. "Could be trimmed up in one afternoon," said Mr. Jarus.

"It's in outrageous condition," said Mrs. Jarus.

She was right enough. Clearly no one had competed in repairs or plantings with the house next door. There was, in fact, no house at all next door, unless you counted a fine, tall stone dwelling with a carriage house and high hedges, a vacant field away.

"When you buy an old house," Mrs. Jarus said to no one special, "you have to see first if the furnace works and if water really comes out of the taps. You look for loose plaster that's about to drop on your head. I'm sure it will."

"Oh, mother," Dirk mourned.

"And that wagonshed would have to come down."

"No, not the wagonshed," said Dirk. Still, she'd said *would* have to, so she must be considering the place. As for really tearing down the wagonshed,

9

that might be prevented later. First, to make sure of the house.

Mrs. Jarus stepped back for another view and said quite unexpectedly, "There *is* something about it."

A hurrah, half yip, half howl, answered that, as if everything were happily settled.

Inside, Mr. and Mrs. Jarus set a good example of how not to rush into major decisions. But Dirk and Marni, with faith that the decision would be made their way, stubbed their toes on the short high stairsteps in a race to pick out their rooms.

Upstairs, each window had something all its own, but Dirk and Marni ended up at the same one, kneeling. Out beyond, they could see it—the meadow with a giant tree and low hawthorns and a tiny shiny stream, and across that, a strip of thicket.

"Have to explore that stuff." Dirk clumped down the stairs and, with their spaniel Pancho rocketing beside him and Marni straggling after, he raced across the lawn, cut through the chinaberry bushes, crossed the field, and reached the meadow.

And then he stopped.

It was a bigness you could breathe, like the bigness of the Great Lakes nearby. But it was a land bigness, a bigness that you could belong to. Its

3 1833 04393 3826

markings of low growth, of stump, of fieldstone, of towering tree—those were something to hold on to, something never to be washed away.

He found paths of pounded clay that matched the color of running rabbits. At the stream, he and Marni shed their sneakers, and with bare rubbery toes, they clutched a wet log to cross. Pancho plunged into the cold stream and waited on the other bank, saving his drenched hair till he could shake it into their faces.

Now they stood in the thicket, where trees struggled high for space and sun. A wild grapevine hung from one, and Dirk tested it. "Look, it's strong," he called, flying out.

Marni took her turn at vine-flying. "Think of it. A live swing."

But Dirk was on to the next discovery. You couldn't stay too long with one. There was too much else to find and you had to find it now. He sniffed the rich and secret air. "Mushrooms?" A hollow log lay near, laced with fungi. "Don't touch it, Marn." He added with dash, "Probably poison." Then he stooped to look inside. "Sh-sh-sh." From the tunnel blackness, two lights shone, spaced like eyes.

Would a wild animal in hiding come out willingly? It seemed not. To see wild animals, people hid in the brush for weeks sometimes. But could you find out what it was, just prodding a little?

Dirk lowered his voice and picked up a length of branch. "You don't have to hurt him, see?" He was on his knees, poking into the log a little.

Marni, watching at the other end, saw a point of fur begin to move her way, and her arms thrashed the air with signals. First came the massive tail with rich black circles, then a muff of a body held up on little sensitive feet—precision instruments made to handle a crawfish or wash a bit of lettuce with finical nicety.

Dirk sprang to Marni's end of the log just in time to see the sharp masked face as the raccoon humped off to cover.

They ran to follow, but the thicket closed ranks to take care of its own. There was a tree root, and Marni stumbled and fell. A magician might have planned it, for when they looked again, there was no raccoon.

For a minute they stood still. Then Dirk said, "I could have touched him."

"I could have, too. Why didn't we?"

12

There was a reason, Dirk knew, but you'd have to turn yourself inside out to get to it. "Well," he said instead, "if that old raccoon got too scared, he might take off and move out of here. Then we'd never see him after Daddy takes the house."

Marni whirled to look into Dirk's face. After Daddy takes the house? How could Dirk know that he would take it?

The thicket was a place she had known forever, like the memory of an old dreamed wish. From the first instant, she had known. Here with the tangled trees, the small secret animals and the taste of earth—here was where she belonged. Yet coming here had been a chancy thing, so chancy that she might easily never have come to it at all.

After Daddy takes the house. She was reminded only that she could lose it—lose the forever thing she had found. "Why?" she said, needing to hope. "Why will Daddy take the house?"

Dirk pulled at a low branch with great aplomb. "Because it's the kind of a house Daddy would take."

Marni's desperate moment passed. "I think so, too."

They started back. Recrossing the stream, they found a path to the abandoned lane they had seen from the car. Then, behind a hawthorn, there appeared a charred fieldstone chimney and the insistent ruin of its attached brick wall.

People had lived there once, the people that built it, maybe, rolling the fieldstones into place from the glaciated land around, sawing up the boards and all, mortaring the bricks. "And then," said Dirk, a little shaken, "it burned down. Clear to the ground."

They left the chimney ruin at last to sit on stumps of a cut woodland. Through a clearing, the big stone house came into full view. "Just one old lady lives in that," said Dirk. "I heard the agent say so. And that old lady wants to sell the farmhouse." He studied the stone house briefly. "It looks as if nobody young ever did live in her place." And he turned to look at the whole great tree.

The tree was the most conspicuous thing in the meadow, but as if they needed to come to it a little at a time, they had saved it for exploring last. Now they slid off their tree stumps and approached it, seeing how the great trunk thrust up its bouquet, an offering to a suitable giant.

"Big," whispered Marni. "It's big!"

A whistle came from the branches, and a cardinal flew down to a low hawthorn. Dirk watched it.

"There'll be nests in a meadow like this." He turned again to the great tree. "That tree has to be mighty old. You'd think a storm would have busted off some branches by now, like on those big ones at home." But, though the lowest limbs reached up with the girth of grown trunks themselves, no torn gap showed on the whole of the tree.

Marni's voice was hushed. "Maybe the tree is enchanted."

They made a half-circle round it, silent, their backs to the hedge of the big stone house. Dirk pointed at the tree trunk just above his head. There in a fold of bark was the tip of a coarse rusty hook. "That's old, that hook. It's almost swallowed up with the trunk growing out. I wonder what that was for, way out here."

Then out of the stillness, they heard a voice. "You look at the tree."

They turned sharply. Behind them stood a gnome of an old man, his bronzed outdoor face just reaching Dirk's shoulder, his remarkable eyes turning first on Marni, then on Dirk. The knees of his work clothes were wet with mud, as if he had been kneeling in it, and he moved with a limp, for an iron scaffold was attached to the shoe of his shorter leg.

16

Marni moved closer to Dirk, and even Dirk stepped back, wary. Still, how could you be afraid of a little old man who needs an iron support just to let him walk? "That's right," said Dirk. "We're looking at the tree. And there's a hook grown into it. Do you know what that's for?"

Now those eyes turned to the tree for a long moment. Then the old man said, "It is a gypsy hook."

Marni looked at Dirk. "A gypsy hook? What does he mean?"

"Do gypsies come here?" Dirk asked.

And Marni, her longing overcoming fear, sighed in a deprived way, "I've never seen the gypsies."

But the old man was not one to stay for their chatter. Already he was on his way to the big stone house, the iron scaffold thudding on the ground. *Da-dud, da-dud,* the sturdy rhythm grew fainter till an opening in the hedge took the sight and the sound of him away.

2. Gold From The Ground

The furnace did work and so did the water system. Both were younger than the house. Craftsmen had built that house a hundred years ago, and even the plaster was sound. The Jaruses moved in.

There was so much to find out about. The first day after school, Dirk checked in and managed to be out the door again before Marni got home, his pockets stuffed with apples.

"You'll have your pockets out of shape," Mrs. Jarus called after him, but it was the sound of habit more than hope.

He loped across the meadow. From the stream, he could see someone stooping at work in the thicket. It was the gnome he and Marni had encountered in the meadow, the gardener at the stone house. The

19

old man was picking up debris of sticks and twigs. "What was he doing that for? Thicket all slicked up could scare the raccoon away."

He called a greeting across the stream, but the old man paid no attention. Dirk came alongside him and began to help fill the basket. Still he was ignored. Then he found a green twig to toss on the heap. At once the old man threw it out.

"Oh," said Dirk, innocently. "Fireplace kindling."

"Stove."

Stove? But no explanation came. Dirk told his name and made a few tries at talk. When the basket was filled at last, the little man straightened his back and looked a long moment at Dirk. Then grudgingly he spoke a name, "Michael." And Dirk saw that he was trusted that much, at least.

Dirk helped carry the weathered bushel basket, and they crossed the log bridge, Michael with surprising sureness. Now they stood in the meadow, facing the sweep of the great tree.

"That's not just any tree," said Dirk. "What about the hook?"

Michael let go of his side of the basket. "Come." And he led the way to the tree. "Here. King of the Gypsies hung the saddle."

"King of the Gypsies? Who told you, Michael?"

"Nobody told. I saw. I was like you. A boy."

"You could watch? From close by?"

As Michael nodded, Dirk observed that he looked toward the charred chimney wall. So that was it. The burned house must have been Michael's. Maybe it burned at night. Maybe he jumped from an up-stairs window and broke his leg and it didn't mend right.

Wishing the old man would talk more, he said, "My grandfather used to go into a gypsy camp. He got to be a friend of the gypsies, and he painted pictures of them." And when that try at conversa-tion failed, he added, "Will the gypsies ever come back here, do you think?"

Michael lifted his shoulders. Either he was too old and wise to predict what might happen, or he didn't care. He seemed to have finished with the subject, for now he sat on a tree stump and took a smooth wooden flute from inside his shirt. Putting it to his lips, he tried a few notes, drawing out fuller ones, and soon the sure tones began to climb the air.

But Dirk, facing the tree with its harness hook and remembering his grandfather's stories, could think only of the gypsies.

The music made it easy. There was a wildness in those oval notes, a wood-bird tone that evoked an imagery—whole trees in place of the decaying stumps; a grove bright with gypsy women's swaying skirts, with autumn leaves, and with flames tearing and crumpling under a campfire kettle. In the wagons, gypsy babies stirred in their sleep. At the giant tree, apart from the lesser horses tied to lesser trees, an Arabian horse (white, he'd have it) curved his mane and arched a foreleg. And from the tree hook, a jewelled saddle hung.

When the music stopped, Michael wiped his lips with the back of his hand and tucked his flute away. Dirk's pictures fell apart, and he blinked, sorting the real from the unreal. The meadow with its clumps of hawthorns, its stream, and its mighty tree, still made a magic of its own, but the gypsies and their wagons had gone, and the grove was only a mass of tree stumps again.

Dirk drew a long breath. "You can surely play that flute, Michael."

Michael did not answer. He looked straight ahead and then, without a word, he got up and started back to the hedge opening, picking up the basket of kindling on the way. Had he forgotten Dirk, forgotten why he had come here in the first place? Or was he offended?

Seeing that the old man carried the filled basket with little trouble, Dirk stayed behind. For a while he walked about, uneasy. He sat down on a tree stump again, tapping the toe of his shoe on the ground, gouging the earth a little. And then his shoe hit an object small and hard, a gleaming edge of something.

With a sharp stone and his fingers, he dug till he had it all. It was a coin about as big as a nickel and the color of the sun. Gold? He rubbed off the clinging earth onto his jacket, and a bit of clay fell from a hole punctured near the rim. A trim bearded profile and strange foreign letters showed on one side of the coin.

There could be a whole chest of gold buried somewhere here. He cast a quick look about. Hawthorns screened him from the big house and from his own house. Marni was safely in town, shopping with her mother. He might go home for a spade, but that would take time and might attract attention. He would make do with what was here.

He searched till he found a wide flat stone. Then he began to dig fast. But an hour later he had turned up no more than snail shells, pebbles, and disgruntled bugs. His hands hurt. His arms ached. He gave up the search for now. But a smooth golden coin lay in his pocket, and his dusty fingers closed over it warmly.

Going home, he took the long way round, passing just outside the hedge of the stone house. The place looked deserted. Then, as he observed the tilt of the handsome French roof with its third-floor windows, he glimpsed someone at a window just below. His impression was of a scrap of a woman with white hair and a gray still face. She seemed to be looking out to the meadow and the thicket beyond, not seeing him, though he was just below.

An eerie feeling washed over Dirk's excitement, and he hurried home to shake it off.

At the farmhouse he was in luck. Everyone was still out. He took his coin to the kitchen tap and scrubbed out the last bits of clay with a vegetable brush. Now the detail showed. The date was clear, in Arabic numerals—1879, but some of the letters around the rim were strange. His father's coin book would tell him something.

He found the volume with some reference books and he began to leaf through it. But this was no place to be. Anybody could come busting in. Marni and his mother must be about due home. He tucked the book under his arm and went upstairs two steps at a time.

In his own room, he slid the old-fashioned bolt on the door and dropped to the floor to examine his coin more closely. The letters suggested Russian signs he'd seen in TV pictures. He'd try the Russian section.

There he found it. The profile was of Nicholas II, the last tsar. On the coin's reverse side was the double-headed eagle holding a sceptre in the claws of one foot and a globe of the world in the claws of the other. In the center was a tiny mounted horseman. It was a five-ruble piece—gold.

How had such a coin come to the meadow? However it had, there must be more hidden somewhere under the earth. Meanwhile, he had a luck piece here, and what a luck piece! He'd keep it a secret, telling no one yet.

3. About The Gypsies

Mrs. Jarus set down a platter of steaming pancakes ringed with tiny brown sausages, to be eaten with spiced apple sauce. "Country breakfast," she called. And she drew back the curtains to let the sun help warm the chilly corners.

Mr. Jarus got to the table first. "Ready, Marni?" for Marni was still occupied with her dolls.

"Something here makes me think of my grandfather's farm," said Mr. Jarus, serving. "The house and the sausages, maybe." His voice dropped to a dream tone. "Those homemade sausages in stuffing for the Thanksgiving turkey. Well. About five pancakes, Marni?"

Marni had counted four stacks of eleven each. "About eleven, please," she directed daintily. And, reserving judgment on her father's childhood, "What did you have for dessert on those Thanksgivings?"

"What did we have for dessert? Pumpkin pies from the woodburning oven. Red raspberries canned with the taste of the sun and the bush in them. Then afterward, all the young cousins got black walnuts and hickory nuts and we smashed them outdoors with stones."

Then he said something to Mrs. Jarus that neither Dirk nor Marni understood in the present connection, pleased though they were to hear it. "We've got to leave the wagonshed just as it is."

"But the wagonshed is—"

"I know. But just as it is."

Mrs. Jarus still had some fight left. "Then never let me see the inside of it."

"Never," Mr. Jarus pledged, and turned again to Dirk and Marni. "Those last scraps of nut stuck in the corners of the shells, those were the sweetest."

Marni looked up at him. "Did you have more fun than Dirk and I do?"

Mr. Jarus chewed and thought. "I can't say. Things are different. But," he turned to Dirk, "what's happened to the old games?"

"Well, at our other house we had kids enough,

28

but there was always grass to keep off. And here there's nobody."

Marni dropped her fork. Nobody?

Dirk hurried on, not noticing her. "But there's the meadow and the thicket. I flushed a raccoon out of a hollow log. Yesterday a pheasant flew up just ahead of me, and after the sun went down, I heard an owl."

Marni, who had been beside him at each of these revelations, squeezed her eyelids tight and shut Dirk out of her own picture in return. "It's so *nice* in the meadow," she murmured.

"The gardener at the stone house told me gypsies used to camp there," Dirk said.

"Oh?" Mr. Jarus looked thoughtful. "The meadow and the woods must have been a good stop—rabbits and pheasants and quail, berries and herbs—if the gypsies weren't chased off."

"The gypsies chased off?" said Marni, indignant. "Why?"

"Well, the old gypsies were a different people, natural wanderers, living close to the earth. They lived the way they knew how to live, keeping to their own ancient nomad customs and tribal laws. So, they kept running afoul of laws they didn't

29

know or didn't care about. It wasn't all happy camping, you know."

"It was black magic," Marni hissed. "Grandfather told us."

"They did get a name for black magic and trickery," said Mr. Jarus. "And the women telling fortunes used to say, 'We do not know books, but we know you better than you know yourselves.'"

Marni shuddered with the deliciousness of it.

"In the end," said Mr. Jarus, "there was bad feeling on both sides. Some countries have been very harsh with the gypsies. To a gypsy, a non-gypsy was usually a *gadjo,* and the word is no compliment. The gypsies thought it a great joke to outsmart a *gadjo.* They were proud to be gypsies. They even had a message code to help other gypsies against the *gadjo.* That was the *patrin.*"

"The *patrin?*"

"Sticks or feathers—and farmers complained of raids on their hen houses—or grass or rags arranged in signals."

"But they did live without getting into trouble, too, didn't they?" said Dirk. "With music and things? I liked our record of Dvorak's Gypsy Songs. Then it had to get sat on."

30

"It was in a dark corner," Marni retorted. "It was you that left it there."

"Oh, yes. Music and dancing were great gypsy talents," said Mr. Jarus. "You know about the gypsy fiddle. There's even a legend that begins, 'In the days when the gypsies had no fiddle—' Gifted gypsies have performed for royalty and led troops in battle, their music was that stirring."

"Did they do anything else?" said Dirk.

"They had an uncanny knowledge of metalwork. Some legends say the gypsies are the sons of the Bible's Tubal-cain, the instructor in brass and iron. The men had little portable forges with goatskin bellows for the women and children to pump. And the gypsies traded horses and trained animals. Some of them work with animals now in circuses."

"In circuses," said Marni, happily. "And where are all the others?"

"Oh, some of them live any way they can—in vacant store fronts in cities—and even dress the old gypsy way. Some gave up the gypsy life and got jobs in factories or wherever they could. And a few still wander—in cars now, instead of wagons."

"Where did they come from in the first place?" Dirk asked.

31

"That's been the question. The gypsies had no written language, so they kept no records of themselves. In Europe it was first thought that they came from Egypt, and so the name, 'gypsies.' But now scholars have traced their language, the old Romany, to India, from a thousand years back, more or less."

Mrs. Jarus nodded. "Dark eyes. And coppery skin."

"Usually."

Marni leaned on one elbow, looking out the window. "Think of gypsies in our own meadow. If they got arrested, I hope they took their fiddles and had a good time in jail. And I hope the gypsy babies didn't go hungry."

A cardinal whistled from a chinaberry bush, and down on Main Street, the bank clock chimed eight. Mrs. Jarus rose. "Just the right moment to start a workday."

And at that moment a workday started. It was a city start, a sound to rout rabbits and pheasants and daydreaming owls, to send them scurrying for fresh cover. It was a sound of lunging machinery, and it came from the direction of the meadow.

4. Marni's Black Magic

They ran to a window. In the thicket across the creek, a bulldozer was smashing down trees.

Dirk and Marni cried out. There was a still moment. Then Mrs. Jarus turned to clear the breakfast table. "I guess it was bound to happen. All that land belongs to the woman in the stone house."

"How can the thicket belong to anyone?" Dirk demanded. It's just wild. It belongs to the rabbits and the pheasants and the raccoon." But he knew well enough to whom the thicket belonged. He was saying only what he would like to believe.

Marni turned to her mother hotly. "And it belongs to Dirk and me. We play in it. Doesn't that make it ours, too?"

It was her father who answered. "Yes, the thicket

34

belongs to you in a way, the way the gypsies made the outdoors theirs, a way you can't measure. But there is a law of property that people have to pay attention to, and that law does measure."

"Measuring," said Marni. "Why does everything have to be measured?" And when no one answered at once, she said again, "Why does it?"

"Marni," said Mrs. Jarus, "you know why. That land *belongs* to the woman in the stone house. She may be selling the thicket for money to live on. She probably sold us this house for the same reason. Whatever the reason, she has the right."

Mr. Jarus started out the door. "Let's go and see what they're up to." And with Dirk and Marni, he started across the back yard and the meadow toward the thicket. C629057 CO. SCHOOLS

Dirk did not say aloud what he feared, but Marni said it. "And now will they come on through the meadow and smash down the gypsies' tree? They'd better not. A gypsy curse will be on them." She clenched her teeth and began in a crone's voice, "May their bones—"

"Marni," her father cut in, "if that's a gypsy curse, stop it. It's not these men's idea to cut down the thicket. It's only their job."

35

"Then they can find another job. And if it's the woman in the stone house that told them to, I hope a black gypsy curse gets her, too. They've *wrecked* our woods!"

Marni had never gypsy-cursed anyone before. No one had ever seemed bad enough for that. And now she waited, terrified at what black magic she might have unleashed.

"Stay here," said Mr. Jarus. "I'll talk to the men." And there in the crunching thicket he questioned the foreman.

The plan, he reported back, was to clear the thicket. A row of houses would be built along the stream.

Dirk braced himself. "The meadow, too?"

No, the meadow and the big tree were to be left undisturbed. That was what the foreman said. But as Mr. Jarus spoke, the tree with the wild grapevine fell, and Marni hid her face.

When she looked up, she said, "I'm going to *see* the woman in the stone house about this." Then she stopped. Not one of them had ever talked to the woman in the stone house. Not one of them except Dirk had so much as caught a glimpse of her. What was she like? Marni had wanted so much to visit that house, but if she went there now, would her gypsy curse go with her? Marni hadn't meant to gypsy-curse anyone at all.

Looking back, she asked meekly, "Could we go in and get the grapevine? Couldn't we hang it in the meadow on the buckeye tree?"

But her father turned her face forward with his hand. That was the way he led her back. Walking across the meadow, only Dirk spoke. "I hope the raccoon got away."

5. A Promise Made

Dirk stood at a window of the fragrant kitchen, eating a warm doughnut. Across the field, he could see Michael's quarters in the carriage house loft. He had not seen Michael since that day they had picked up kindling and Michael had talked about the harness hook. Maybe Michael would tell more about seeing the gypsies, if he could be found working around the place.

Dirk started out the door. A late spring coolness had moved down over the Great Lakes, and he had to hurry across the field to keep warm. He saw no sign of Michael, but near the opening of the hedge behind the stone house, he came face to face with someone else. It was the woman he had seen at the upstairs window.

She started sharply, as if she were unused to seeing anyone in that life of hers at the stone house. Yet her response seemed too sharp even for the unexpected. It was more as if she had seen the impossible, as if she had seen a ghost.

Dirk, seeing eyes with trouble and unbelief in them, hurried to tell her his name and his errand. Her answer did not come at once, and when it came, the voice made him think of wood, powdery dry and flaking off with use.

"The Jarus boy?" she repeated. "I almost thought —" her voice trailed off. "Michael is not here. No."

Dirk thanked her and turned, but she called after him in a sort of urgency. "But I am glad to see you. Don't go. There is some cake in the kitchen. Would you like some?"

Stuffed with doughnuts, Dirk would still have welcomed a chance to see inside the stone house, but after this strange encounter, his words stuck and his feet dragged.

"Please come in." And he saw that though her eyes looked anxious, they were gentle, too. He followed her up to the high back steps and through a service porch to the kitchen. "I suppose it's warmer in this room," she said.

She invited him to sit at a table, and while the tea brewed, she placed a silver fork and spoon and an expertly mended linen napkin before him. The slice of pound cake came to him on a frail china plate. Dirk watched as she opened a tall cupboard and took out two china cups with gilt handles and handpainted forget-me-nots—girl cups for a girl drink. He felt trapped.

They sat silent. Finishing his dry pound cake, Dirk looked up and knew she had been studying him. At once she put her cup down and managed a small smile. "Tell me," she said, "do you like your farmhouse?"

"Oh, yes." He liked the big rooms with the high ceilings and the little stairsteps and the slant-roof attics where you could walk on the floor studding if you ducked your head.

Her small unexpected smile said she knew about houses like that.

His mother, he said, liked the big kitchen and the pantry. (She called it the "butt'ry." That was a farm word.) His father liked to call the big front room the "parlor." And there was also a big sitting room, with a bedroom right off that. It was funny and it was nice.

40

"This is an old house, too," she said. "Would you like to see it?"

Willingly now, he followed her through a room-size serving pantry. She opened the door to the diningroom. Instantly, the chill of it struck him, as if he had entered an underground cave. Dark panelling, carved furniture, and glum-faced portraits surrounded him, on guard.

Dust lay deep, and once he looked back and saw his footprints brightening the pattern of the Oriental rug. In the library were walls of books, their leather bindings ragged with years, and they were all wedged together so tightly they looked as if they would pinch the fingers that tried to dislodge them, as crawdads pinched when you picked them up.

The music room held a grand piano and many little giltframed chairs with seats done in needlepoint. There were numerous fireplaces, but no fire. No fire was even laid. And surely no heat was coming from below. He shivered. Maybe she'd let him build her a fire. But then he decided not to ask.

They came at last to an upstairs room. This must be where he had seen her standing. This must be where she stayed. At once his eyes were drawn to a

portrait over the fireplace. It was of a boy about his own age, wearing coat and trousers of a long time past. Someone young had probably lived here, after all, then. Who was it? But his unspoken question was diverted by one of her own.

"Sometimes I see a little girl out there. Is she your sister?"

"Yes," he said. "It's Marni." And to punish her a little for the ruin of the thicket, he added, "We liked the thicket. A raccoon lived there."

The look of a shadow crossed her face. At once he was sorry, and to try to make amends, he said, "But there's still the meadow."

Then in a surer voice than before, she said, "There will be a meadow for you as long as I live here. That much I promise."

Dirk's quick smile thanked her. They turned to the door and went down the circular staircase, their fingers dusting a strip of carving.

The wide door of the front hall stood before them. She tried to open it, but seemed to have forgotten the combination of locks and bolts that held it, so Dirk helped.

"Come back," she said, "and bring your sister." And she called after him, "You will come back?"

Yes, he said, and thanks, he would. But for now, he was glad to escape the cold house with its lone occupant. Only when he was out in the sun did he feel able to look back. She was standing at a long silk-draped window, and she waved to him.

6. An Owl Missing

The meadow was spared. Things happened as the workmen had said, and as the woman in the stone house promised. The great tree went unharmed. The stream flowed as before, and the hawthorns and briars grew just a little wilder.

But now from across the meadow came the patterned sound of hammer blows—*one, two, three, four, five, six, seven. One, two, three, four, five.* The new houses followed the curve of the stream. Soon roofers, plumbers, furnace men and electricians moved along the line, adding their work to each shell.

Figuring out which room was which might be a sort of game while the walls were only sketched in, Dirk thought, and when the workmen had left for

45

the day, he and Marni crossed on the log bridge. They found a kind of excitement in the raw wood fragrance hanging on damp air, but even Marni found the guessing game too easy. Unlike their farmhouse, so full of odd surprises and cubbyholes, the floor plans here were all exactly alike, merely reversed for every second house.

Dirk looked at them in distaste. "I suppose the people in them will be all alike, too."

Marni, chin in hands, hung her shoulders out an unpaned side window, facing an identical window in the next house. Between these two buildings, where she had picked bluets and spring beauties a few weeks ago, lay an ooze of yellow earth.

"Remember the screech owl?" she said.

"Sure. He sounded so little and fierce and scared of himself."

And Marni said, "I never hear that little screech owl any more."

7. The Meadow Crowd Under Ground

The new houses were all painted white. No tree, no tangle was left of the thicket. But across the stream was the meadow with the hawthorns, the meadow with the great tree.

One by one, the houses were filled. Bicycles and red wagons strewn about said that young families had come to live there. Hairlike spears of green began to brush the brown hauled-in topsoil. Signs of ownership appeared. Snappish ones read "Keep Off The Grass"; playful ones, "Your Feet Are Killing Me"; and prayerful ones, just "PLEASE." The grass grew beautifully. It was fed and sprayed and mowed and clipped and kept off. It was grownups' grass. The child grass was in the meadow.

So the thicket had gone, but summer was good,

for out of the houses, children ran. They ran in a gamut of sizes, shapes and dispositions, and Dirk was reassured.

Nearest in age to Dirk and Marni were Han and Linda Porter. The four drifted together for the first time at the chimney wall.

"What's this old thing?" said Linda, holding back her pink butterfly skirt from the charred bricks.

Marni's dark eyes warned her. "That's our ancient ruins."

"It's junky. Why doesn't somebody tear it down?"

Count ten, Marni, her father had once prescribed for such crises, but when that solved nothing, Marni turned to Dirk. "You tell her."

And Dirk said, "Why would you tear it down, for Pete's sake?"

Han looked at his young sister without enthusiasm. "Sure. Where'd you ever get one of those again if you tore it down? Who'd tear it down, anyway? Girls, maybe, always cleaning things up."

"Not me," said Marni, feeling the sting of unfairness. But Han was on to fresh grandeurs.

"That's a big old tree over there. Hey, Dirk. Race you to it!" It was a tied race, and they braced themselves against the tree trunk, getting their

49

breath. Dirk showed Han the gypsy harness hook, and when Han seemed rightly impressed, Dirk had other meadow treasure to show. He took the coin from his pocket, telling how he had come upon it, sharing it for the first time.

Han turned it over. Then he looked at Dirk, the tree, and the reach of meadow. "You know something, Dirk? You know something, Jarus? It's O.K. here."

Two other boys approached. Spook, a meagre lad with blue shadows under his eyes, whistled up into the tree.

Rocco, the wide one, was not so artless. "I seen trees big as that. Bigger."

"Where?" said Spook, ready to believe.

"In Texas. In my own front yard. We had all kinds."

Dirk studied Rocco briefly for signs of fraud. "This one's an elm. And you know what's happening to elms? They're dying. Like flies."

"That's right." Han nodded. "Like flies."

"And you know how old this tree is?" said Dirk. "It's about a hundred and fifty years old."

"You'd think if the tree was that old, it'd rot up," Spook said respectfully.

50

Rocco kicked the tree base. "Prob'ly rotten inside."

Dirk and Rocco stood eye to eye and Dirk's words hit back. "This is no rotten tree. Look how thick the leaves are up there. And green."

"O.K., O.K.," said Rocco. "How do you know it's a hundred and fifty years old?"

"You can't tell for sure. You figure by its size."

"You can so tell," Rocco sailed a stick a handsome distance. "You can count the rings in the trunk."

"Sure you can if you can count," said Han. "But that's after it's cut down."

Dirk chewed a sour clover leaf. "That's right, Rocco. Only after it's cut down."

✿   ✿   ✿

Exhausted from games and from hurdling tree stumps, the meadow crowd gathered under the big tree. Dirk rolled the coin in his hand.

"There have to be more of those coins in this meadow," Han said.

"If we could just figure out the right place to dig. I dug all around where I found this. I found an Indian flint. And they find little fossils in the shale around here. Old as old."

"About a hundred thousand years, I'll bet," said Rocco.

"Millions."

"Millions of *years*?"

"More than three hundred millions."

There was a silence, and Rocco spoke into it. "That's too many years to get excited about. Didn't you find any more money?"

"No. Maybe if we all dug, though—"

"All of us together—"

Who could tell? Buried gold, Indian flints, tomahawks, fossils were probably lying in the earth just under their feet this minute. They made their plans.

Next morning Dirk and Marni were up and outdoors early, and in minutes the meadow crowd began to hurry out.

"Spades are the best," Dirk had advised, but forks and shovels came from the garages as well. The smallest children came along with kitchen gear. Screen doors were held thoughtfully, not to slam, and there was a rush to the meadow.

"With treasure," Dirk said, "you'd think they'd bury it somewhere around the big tree, to find it again. We got to think like pirates. Thirty paces out from the biggest root hump or something."

"Wonder how far the roots go," said Rocco. "We wouldn't get much dug out if we kept bumping into tree roots. Without machinery, that is."

"Machinery! For Pete's sake," said Dirk. "Tell you what. Let's get out past the dripline—that's the farthest place for rain to drop off the leaves—that way we ought to be sure."

Han lifted his arms and closed his eyes, swaying. "Which way?"

"Just on a hunch," said Dirk, "how about that biggest root pointing southeast?"

So the place was fixed. At first the going was easy, but below the topsoil they hit heavy yellow clay. The Jarus pancake turner broke first. Marni looked at the ruin in her hands. Still, if it took ten allowances to replace, it had been worth it. She was a part now of something glorious.

Only Dirk and the older boys with heavy implements made progress now, and that was slow. By nine o'clock they had a shallow beginning. Dirk slapped his forehead with a heroic red bandana. Now the others could admit to blisters, aching muscles, and hollow stomachs.

Dirk moved his arms and shoulders with care. "We could come back tomorrow."

"Same time, same place?" said Han.

"Same time, same place," came the chorus.

Each daybreak now, Dirk and Marni woke the others to go digging. In the end, no fossils, no Indian artifacts, and certainly no buried treasure had been turned up, but they had a deep wide pit in the ground, useful in itself. By now they were all members of the Club Forever. The Pit became their clubhouse, and the handmade hill beside it, the Lookout.

Seeds of coarse meadow grass sprouted on their hill, and Dirk, standing against a clay wall of the Pit, traced the new green curve above. "You know what? That hill looks built right into the meadow. We changed the big old earth. We really changed it."

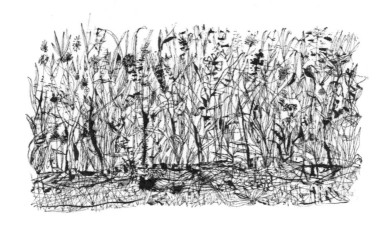

8. Intruder In The Meadow?

Hot winds of midsummer blew in off the Great Plains, but the Jarus farmhouse was ample and airy. The new houses, cramped on lower ground, stored the heat and kept it through the night, only to have it build up to new levels the next day.

In the farmhouse Dirk rummaged in a shelf closet. "Where's the army blanket?"

Mrs. Jarus hurried over to prevent disaster. "In the big cedar chest, naturally, to keep the moths out. What in the world do you want with the army blanket in this weather? Dirk, watch out! You're jumbling everything out of order."

"Sorry, Mom. I need the army blanket. We're going to sleep in the meadow. Everyone's room stays hot all night."

"Our rooms don't. That's one reason we took this house."

"I know, but in the Club Forever we share and share alike. So I can either invite them all to sleep in my room, or I can sleep in the meadow with them. But I'd rather sleep on the ground."

Mrs. Jarus seemed to implore the ceiling for strength. "And parents toil to provide roofs for their young. All right. Take the blanket. But don't bring it in tomorrow. Hang it on the line for airing and brushing. And before you come inside, brush yourself off, too. I don't want any ants or crickets or lizards or mud or grass in the house. Hear?"

"Oh, Mom, a little mud and crickets and lizards won't hurt anybody."

"Just keep them out of this house."

Marni came by in time to get the drift of the plans.

"Good. And I'll take my top quilt."

"Certainly you will not," said Mrs. Jarus.

"No girls," Dirk growled. "Girls are invited to stay home."

Marni tramped off to her own room. Dirk was the one who was getting the chance to sleep in the meadow. Sometimes when she'd been shut out of things, he used at least to say, "Sorry, Marn." It never had changed anything, but it helped her feelings.

She clicked her door shut. In her mirror she fancied herself the mother of a boy who had just brought crickets and lizards and mud and even grass into the house. With all this fancied litter and boy, she dealt smartly, saying her words extra clear, all behind closed teeth.

At dusk that night, the boys gathered in the meadow, carrying blankets and, in case hunger struck, milk and pop, sandwiches, cake, fruit, cookies and chocolate bars. Hunger struck early, then one by one the shifting humps grew quiet till only Dirk and Han lay awake.

To the west of overhead, stars faded in the floodlight of a setting moon. The meadow was a refuge from the stored heat of indoors, but still no breeze stirred. The strident energy of crickets withered. The katydids' abrasive cheerfulness turned to feuding. *Did, didn't.*

Dirk lay on his back. "After such a hot day, even a full moon looks different. Kind of limp."

"Sure does. What do you s'pose makes it look like that?"

"Something about the atmosphere, I guess."

Han raised his head with caution. "A night like this, what do you s'pose they're all rolled up in their blankets for?"

"I don't know. Makes them feel safer, maybe."

"This old meadow ought to be safe enough. Who'd want the meadow? Excepting us?"

"Sure. Funny how at night everything looks different, though. You think you know every inch of this meadow, and you don't, at all. Those little thorn trees over there, don't they look bigger?"

Han considered, yawning. "Hey, they do look bigger. They sure do."

The moon dropped below the trees as if in relief at going. In the richer darkness a tree frog trilled.

"Han? Hey, Porter?"

But Han had rolled over on his blanket, and Dirk knew that he alone lay awake. Around him, black sky reached to earth. Stars and distant street lights threw everything into a sort of sculpture. The hawthorns looked twice as big and, as if night gave them a provable secret life, Dirk saw them moving toward him in stealth.

When trees creep toward you like that, you don't feel like yourself, he thought. You don't even think

59

the same way. No wonder so many scare stories came out of forest lands. With trees at night, you could think you were in some impossible place with impossible things happening.

Shivering, but not with cold, Dirk pulled up his blanket. One by one, the katydids used up their sound, wind-up toys run down. The stillness hung between earth and sky, hung tall, timeless and listening. It was a kind of waiting. What for? He didn't know. His eyeballs burned—he hadn't blinked. His neck ached.

It must be hours since the moon went down. Now did the east look a little less black? Softly a grayness spread. If he took his eyes off the fading North Star, could he find it again? He'd try.

He dropped his focus to the low-growing trees. Their aggressive look was gone. They stood meekly back at their daytime posts as if nothing at all had happened. And then across the meadow in the V between two huddled hawthorns, he thought he saw someone moving. In an instant, even that glimpse was lost in leaves.

Was Spook up, looking for rabbits? Dirk rolled over and counted boys. All were there, and though Spook's face was under his blanket, the thinnest roll with blond hair-sprigs at one end had to be Spook.

A prowler in the meadow? He'd rather believe that someone had broken into his own room. The drumbeat inside his ribs began to block out everything else. His arms and legs felt locked in deep freeze. And yet he knew it wasn't simple fear. It was something about the meadow and how the meadow was a special place, a place for the meadow crowd alone. Someone merely passing through it for a short-cut would leave it something less.

Should he waken Han? Should he rouse the others? No. An hour ago the trees had looked for all the world as if they moved. What he had just seen must have been another illusion. That's what it was, all right, an illusion. He'd say nothing to the others. He'd just watch.

But the second night Dirk was already worn out with watching. He slept till daylight. For the others it was still early, but he found Spook sitting up. "How come you're awake, Spook?"

"Who wants to get ate up with mosquitoes? I been slapping mosquitoes all night."

Dirk plucked a tuft of grass. "See anyone?"

"Saw a rabbit."

"I mean somebody."

61

"No, I didn't see anybody. Who would I see? Nobody but us ever goes in the meadow." Spook frowned and hunched forward to study Dirk's face. "Do they?"

"No, I guess not. Of course not. Nobody but us."

✿   ✿   ✿

The children had come from the crowded cities, and if you had asked them what was the best thing about the edge of the little city, they would have answered at once, "The meadow." The best thing about the edge of the city was not the city, they would say, but what was left of the country. They would be thinking then of the tree with the old gypsy harness hook, of the Pit and the Lookout, and the chimney wall.

They would be thinking of the tiny shiny stream and of the skater bugs streaking solemnly over the top of it; the stream where Dirk had shown them how to catch crawdads, scooping them up with a little sand to blunt their pinching.

They would be thinking of the young dandelion greens they slipped into their egg sandwiches for the fine firm feeling of living off the land; of the wild strawberries they crushed on their tongues for the ecstasy of juice piercing sweet and sour all at the same instant.

They would think of the rabbit's nest, lined with fur and stuffed with limp-eared young ones that Dirk allowed no one to touch nor Pancho to sniff, till one dawn they would find that the rabbits had grown up and gone.

They would think of the rivulets of rain testing, testing, searching for a soft place in the earth to wear away a path to join the tiny stream and with it, a bigger stream, and a bigger one still. How they all longed with Dirk to do that, to follow the tiny stream all the way to Lake Erie, to rush with the torrents of Niagara into Ontario, and with the sparkling St. Lawrence out to sea.

This was the meadow. The hawthorns grew low, and Dirk taught them all, even the youngest, to play Run Sheep Run. Gathering for a delicious game at dusk, crouching behind the hawthorns or the old chimney wall or the giant tree, they listened for their captain's signals across the meadow, all in secret code to mean, "Run this way, run that way, run for cover, now come out, only keep out of sight. Run hard, run fast and *now*, run to Home, oh, get Home, little sheep, for our side must win the game."

The little sheep tripped and stumbled over the roots and clods in the moonlight, their hearts beating wild and desperate, their sides aching, for they must win, they must win for their captain and their team—till the parents blew their whistles to come in. It was late, late, even for a white summer night.

9. Triumph In The Tree

"Could be a great tree house up there." The meadow crowd had gathered around Dirk. "If you could just line up a couple of angles to hold a board. Even one little bitty old board. And if you could figure out how to get up there."

All the bigger boys had tried climbing the tree. One heavy branch grew below the main fork, but it was far below. The tree was too big to grasp around, and it offered no gnarls to catch at.

"From the top of a ladder we could do it," said Dirk. "We could throw a rope over a limb and climb the rope."

Cheers went up and faded abruptly.

"Where'd we get a ladder?"

"Or a rope?"

"Or any boards for a tree house?"

"That's simple. In our wagonshed. There's all kinds of stuff in there."

"Then let's get going."

The wagonshed, as they approached it, looked prim enough. It was painted white and the doors were closed, as always. Now as Dirk swung them open, a reverent whistle rose.

Dirk thought of other garages he'd seen—mower, rake, clippers. Where equipment was more adventurous, a shelf would hold hammer, screw driver, wrench and pincers, all laid parallel like a silver place setting for a Fathers' and Sons' Banquet. He looked at the faces of his friends, and it pleased him to be generous. "It's all up for grabs."

Still no one moved. It was that beautiful.

There were odd bits of wood left from a hundred efforts, suggesting birdhouses, doghouses, dollhouses, shelves and chests and model airplanes, none of them pre-cut. There were props from old school plays, furniture that might be repaired, furniture that might not, fence wire and screen, and nuances of glues. There were old wheels in assorted sizes, tires, picture-frame molding, paint, brushes, wooden orange crates and various sizes of rope.

66

There were river rocks for flagstones, flower pots, fieldstones, a roaster lid and an occasional brick.

Some of this wealth had been brought in lately by the Jaruses. Some had been left by the people who had lived there before, and perhaps before, and before, for in places it was layered, magnificent as the ancient cities of Troy built one on top of the other.

There was little that any adult of tidy thinking and sound mind would place in the arms of a moving man, yet each item was exactly right for some use or another.

Spook's voice dropped to a hush. "Gee-ee!"

Han scratched his ribs and dreamed aloud. "Everything's sort of like the first piece of a puzzle. You start thinking what you'd put with it."

Dirk met these tributes with modesty. He kicked a pile of lumber. "The way those branches slant, we'd have to fit wedges in. What we could do, we could take some of this studding and saw through it catty-cornered."

"And we can take a hammer up and nail the studding good to the tree." Spook left the ground in a leap so astonishing that it seemed he might waft on up, weightless, without need of a ladder.

68

Still, they dragged one to the tree, with a stout length of rope to knot for climbing.

Han and three boys of Spook's age held the ladder, one at each shaft, and Dirk started up with the rope. At each step he could feel the determined steadying, like a shudder. Two steps from the top would be high enough, all right, if you wanted to stay in one piece. He could brace his shins against the first step from the top and hold on with his left hand while he swung.

The rope was bundlesome. He amassed the coils on the ladder top, gathered loops in his right hand, and gauged his distance. "Ready?"

The ground crew leaned harder against the shafts. "Throw!" Dirk's balance shifted and the ladder swung to the right. For a split second he lost his footing, but he clutched, groped, and somehow got it back again. The rope had missed.

Dirk looked things over. "Maybe if everybody would help steady it." And everybody did, the blue jeans with their wide stances like a cathedral's flying buttresses, hooked oddly together, side by side, for support.

The next try succeeded. The rope's short end was worked down over the limb till both ends hung

69

near the ground. There they were tied together and Dirk began the climb.

By the time he reached the roped limb, he was winded, but he forced together his last scraps of strength and swung himself into the fork. For now, that was all. He sat in the heady height, getting his breath back, letting sensations wash over him. Any leafy tree of a decent size was worth a climb, but something was different here. This shelter, like the meadow floor each morning, became a whole world he had just found, and found first of anyone. An appropriate other-worldly feeling brushed his head. It was the flutter of a million tiny leaf fans, lifting his hair at the roots.

Not till moments later did he look on up into the tree. And then he knew. A tree house here was all but impossible. You'd be lucky to find a place for a single plank. And it felt even higher than it looked. Alone, he thought wistfully, he might have managed it. But all the others were younger. Some, like Marni, were a lot younger. You had to think of things like that.

"What about it, Jarus? What are you up there so long for?"

It was like fighting your way alone through every

70

hardship to the North Pole, only to get a radioed message: COME HOME AT ONCE. URGENT.

Slowly he turned his back on the tree world and worked himself down to report his findings face to face. "Elms don't really grow right for tree houses. We could keep the rope just to get up into the fork, though. Except the littlest ones."

Marni was one of the littlest ones. She could have been boosted up for a start, but Dirk held out a half-promise instead. "Wait till next summer, Marn. You might be a better size then."

So the tree house never came to be, but in the elm there was already a tree house of another kind. It was a hanging basket woven out near the end of a lateral branch. Sometimes there was a flash of black and orange near it, and the vigorous call of an oriole.

10. A Promise Withheld

Day after day in those hot weeks, the great tree gave comfort. The shadow of it swung from west in the morning to east in the evening. The new houses seemed like a row of white beds with fevered children in them, and the tree saying, "Be patient. I will come to you soon to touch you with cool fingers."

At noon the remarkable shadow, though trunkless now, was still so generous that it sheltered a house where the stream curved.

And day after day the stone house stood apart, its lone occupant out of sight.

At home Dirk said, "I have to go to the stone house for a visit. I promised." But for all the swagger of his words, he was apprehensive. His only visit stayed with him in a way he wanted to shake off and couldn't. Perhaps if he went now and kept his promise and got it over with (that was his mother's way of dealing with sticky problems) he'd be free of all that.

It was worth a try. "You could come along, Marn. She asked me to bring you. You're even invited."

"I am? Oh. Oh, wait. I'll have to change to my new shoes. Should I wear a skirt—and have a hair ribbon, like Linda?"

And then she remembered. Once she had stormed across the meadow with a gypsy curse for the men who were cutting down the thicket. Her father stopped her before she really said it, but it was a bad thing she had wanted to do, a thing to hurt other people. And after that she'd even hoped a gypsy curse would get the woman in the stone house. Marni dropped to the floor and covered her face. "I can't go."

"What do you mean, you can't go? What are you crying about?"

"I can never go to the big stone house. I can never." And that was all Marni would say.

So Dirk went alone, the sun's heat drilling into his flesh as he crossed the field.

At the big front door, he waited full minutes. At last the door opened. She looked smaller, it seemed to Dirk, and her face was sort of like her teacups —translucent.

She was wearing a winter scarf, and as before, she seemed to be brushing away the telltale bits that clung to her from her singular world. But whatever the effort, she said, "It's good of you to come and see me." And the way she said it, it didn't sound like just a glassy grownup thing to say.

She led the way through the gloom and dust to the upstairs sitting room. There was a little sunshine here, and you could look out at the big tree. It seemed important to him to locate the gypsies' hook on it, and when he had, he said, "I wish I could have seen the gypsies out there."

Each time she spoke, her words came late, after he thought she would not speak at all. "Michael told you about the gypsies?"

"Yes, he told me."

"They made a pretty sight. We used to watch them from here. Sometimes we visited the camp. There was never any trouble. When they stopped coming to the meadow, we missed them."

It was like the barest outlines on TV news. You

knew there was more, but you knew you weren't going to hear it. He'd have to hear it all piecemeal. Well, Michael had watched the gypsies, too. Michael might tell him more. And for something to say, he said, "Michael's been here a long time, hasn't he?"

"Yes, he came here when there were horses in the carriage house. He looked after them. We all liked Michael."

"Was he in the house when it burned?"

She looked perplexed. "When the house burned?"

"The house in the meadow where the chimney stands."

"Michael never lived in that house. Michael lived—" She trailed off into vagueness, seeming to search her memory. "Michael lived nearby."

She seemed tired. It was time to go. But when Dirk left, she spoke with the very words from which he'd hoped to free himself in coming here today.

"You will come back?"

It had been hard enough to keep his first promise, and Dirk hedged about a second one.

He'd try, he said.

11. Gold And The Message Of A Rag

Michael was digging up plantain near the carriage house and dropping it into a small handmade basket. Dirk considered the weed-studded grass plot. "Want some help?"

The old man shook his head over the half-dozen plants he had dug up and jerked his hand toward the stone house. "She tells me, 'Weed.' For today, enough." He carried the basket to a shaded bench and sat down. Then he took his knife and cut the coarse leaves of the plantain from the ropy roots.

"Why do you do that?"

"I do not eat the roots."

Phrases from his father rang back. "Close to earth." "Herbs and berries." He looked freshly at Michael's deep skin tones and dark eyes. Michael had lived "nearby," the woman in the stone house had said. And Michael was not quite at home with English.

"The woman in the stone house," he began carefully, "said she missed the gypsies when they stopped coming to the meadow. Why do you suppose they stopped?"

Michael threw plantain roots to the ground. "It was a bad time for gypsies."

"A bad time? How was it bad?"

"For gypsies, it was never easy, but this was bad."

"What did they do then?"

Had he asked too much? Would Michael get up and leave him again, taking his story with him? But Michael stayed.

Then he said, "The King of the Gypsies called the people. 'The *gadjo* wants all things from the factories,' the King said. 'The *gadjo* wants nothing from the gypsies. No mended pots, only new pots from the factories. Gypsies cannot trade horses,' the King said. 'Machines are the horses.' "

It was the most that Dirk had ever heard him say at once, and now he waited.

After a minute Michael went on. " 'The little work in the fields,' the King said, 'what is that? Gypsies are not made to be farmers,' " and the old man spat on the ground. "The King said, 'Gypsy women cannot even tell fortunes. The police come and arrest them.' " And he fingered the plantain leaves expertly—for their tenderness, Dirk guessed.

"The King said, 'Gypsies must live. Gypsies must get jobs like the *gadjo* and become house-gypsies.' " Michael was shaking, his eyes on the ground. Then he recited the final indignity. "The King said, 'Gypsy children must even go to school and learn from books.' "

Michael raised his head and looked toward the meadow. "Out there our King said this."

Our King. So at last he had said it. Their eyes met like the eyes of conspirators. Then, thought Dirk, the woman in the stone house wasn't confused at all. She was keeping the secret of Michael's origin for him, once she learned it was a secret. But for now, there was more to learn about the gypsies. He leaned forward. "And then?"

"We stamped out the campfire. My people went to the wagons. They did not come back."

"But you stayed?"

Michael paused a moment. "When I am old, the gypsies will come for me."

Old? Dirk said, "You didn't want me to know this before."

"The *gadjo* does not like the Gypsies." He hunched his shoulders. "O.K. The gypsies do not like the *gadjo*."

"He tells me this," Dirk said to himself. "He trusts me. I guess I'm not a *gadjo* to him." And he returned the compliment. "The gypsies were pretty smart, managing so long to live the way they did."

Michael's eyes grew lively. He straightened his back and thumped his chest. "No school, no book, but the gypsy is smart with the *gadjo*. And to be hungry, that was nothing. Gypsies help other gypsies."

"I know. With *patrin*."

Michael seemed not to hear.

"With *patrin*—the sticks and things they worked into messages for other Gypsies."

Still Michael sat there as if he'd never heard of it. At last Dirk said flatly, "I wish I knew some *patrin*."

The old man studied Dirk's face. Then with an abrupt move, he got up. Dirk expected him to stalk off again, but instead the little gypsy said, "I will show you *patrin*."

80

Dirk followed him to the meadow. There Michael pulled up a tuft of coarse grass and left it upturned. "You find the grass. Gypsies were here." He looked at the high little cirrus clouds and felt the underside of the clod. "Today in the sky it is dry. Yesterday was rain. So, the grass is dry, but not *under* the grass." He drew his conclusion. "*Today,* maybe, gypsies were here. Maybe you could find gypsies down the road there."

Then he took out his hunting knife, cut two strips of bark from a bush and tied them to the buckeye tree, to hang at Dirk's eye level.

"What does that mean?"

"A bad stopping place."

"What's bad about it?"

Michael shrugged. "The house over there might not like gypsies, might keep a biting dog, might call the police. What matters? No gypsy should knock on that door."

Farther on he took a twig from a tree, pared a strip of bark to hang down, and stuck the twig upright in the ground. Then he went through the motions of judging—the feel of the stripped twig for dampness, skillfully weighed against weather conditions. The conclusion, "Fresh *patrin*."

81

"And the direction the strip hangs in, that means something, too?" said Dirk, sure that he had the feel of it now.

The little gypsy flashed him a crafty look and said only, "Two pieces hanging mean something else." Then he pulled out a tail of his own weathered shirt and tore a strip from it. He chose a hedge twig, again at Dirk's eye level, and tied the rag in a circle around it. "Here a gypsy woman could maybe tell a fortune. She could get a dollar."

Short of breath from his efforts, Michael sat down on a large fieldstone. Dirk sat near, feeling a good glow to be trusted with secrets of the *patrin* of so ancient a race. What could he share with Michael in return? His own secret, surely—the coin he kept in his pocket.

Michael took the coin and weighed it in his palm as if he dealt in these matters every day. "Gold." Then he examined it closely and pointed across the meadow. "Over there you found it."

Was this some gypsy divination? Dirk knew he had been well screened from sight that day. "How did you know?" he asked.

Michael reached into his own pocket and brought out a second coin.

"But it's just like mine," Dirk said. "Even the hole in it is the same. Even the date."

Michael nodded. "In old Russia I was a boy and I could play the flute—even such a young boy. My father could play the fiddle. We made music for a friend of the tsar. The friend gave a bag of rubles to my father. To me, a small boy, he gave two ruble pieces."

"And then?"

"We came to America. I was a young man. I took my rubles to make earrings for a young girl. But out there I lost one earring."

Questions crowded Dirk's mind about Michael's youth, about the gypsies, about old Russia, about the young girl. Was there a tall and handsome gypsy who had two earrings to give her, perhaps? But for now, there was nothing that Dirk felt privileged to ask.

For now, the thing was the golden coin. For months he had transferred it from pocket to pocket, always sure to carry it with him. How many times he had felt its burnished surface on his palm. He'd miss it now. And he held out his hand to give it back.

Michael waved him off. "Keep the rubles. They

bring you luck—*bakht,* the old gypsies say." And then with a quick move, Michael offered his own coin. "Here. You take mine. I take yours."

They made the exchange. It was a ritual of two who might have been enemies, but who had made friends instead. A little festive, a little solemn, the moment grew. Then Dirk said, "About the *patrin.* It's all right if I show the meadow crowd?"

An inward look came over the ancient face. "Some gypsies need the *patrin,*" Michael muttered. "Police arrest the gypsies." And then with an off-hand gesture, he cancelled out what he had said. "So tell. I did not show you real *patrin.* With the *patrin* I showed, police could not find the gypsies."

"I would never do anything to hurt the gypsies," Dirk protested.

But he had spoiled something and he knew it, for now Michael put distance between them again, a distance that said. "Only I am a gypsy. Never you."

✧　　✧　　✧

Whose meadow was it?

By summer's end you might have stopped any young person in the new houses to ask. And no doubt he would have answered in surprise, "But it's no one's meadow. It's just wild." Of all the meadow crowd, Dirk alone had called at the big stone house.

The smallest and most faithful of Dirk's followers might have said, "It's Dirk's meadow. He was here first. He told about the gypsies' tree. He found a real gypsy and a gold coin that the gypsy lost in the meadow and an Indian flint. He thought up the Pit and the Lookout and the tree rope.

"He knows everything in the meadow. He showed us the wild strawberry blossoms, so we could tell where the berries would come and not step on any. He found the meadowlark's nest in the grass, and we all stayed away till the young ones could fly. He showed us the oriole's woven basket way out at the edge of the big tree.

"He showed us how to play Run Sheep Run and he lets all of us play, even the little ones. If the meadow has to belong to someone, it ought to belong to Dirk."

Dirk did not think of the meadow as his. He was not so young as that. He would have said, "The meadow and the big tree belong legally to the woman in the stone house, but they are for all of us. She promised."

And now the blue and white of chicory and Queen Anne's lace had made way for wild flowers gold and purple. The hawthorns yielded their puckered dwarfs of apples, as bewilderingly dry and bitter to bite into as the things that parents like. The teasel had been gathered and dyed for the mothers' winter arrangements of weeds. The autumn crop of buckeyes, polished for trading, rattled in pockets.

It was an October morning when Michael came to the Jarus house, his eyes filled with trouble. "Come with me," he said to Mr. Jarus. "Come."

When Mr. Jarus returned, his face was grave. He put one hand on Marni's shoulder and one on Dirk's. "The woman in the stone house," he said, "is dead."

12. A Note In Patrin

A few weeks later, a scarlet sedan stood in the
drive of the stone house. Dirk saw it as he went
past on his bicycle.

"What do you think is going to happen over
there?" he asked when he got home.

Mrs. Jarus lifted a pot lid and added a pinch of
herbs. "Let's hope that someone buys it to keep just
as it is. So many of these fine old places are torn
down to make way for modern buildings."

"They'd tear down the big stone house?" Dirk
rallied his hopes. "I saw a man bring some people
to look at it yesterday. And there's a red car there
now. I'd better talk to Michael tomorrow."

In the night a storm broke. Wind sheared the
leaves of the maples at the stone house. Next

87

morning Dirk ran over a bright wet layer of them. Summer had gone and so, hastily, had autumn.

Rounding the hedge, he saw that the red car had left. Good. He could speak to Michael freely. Maybe this time the house had been sold. Maybe the new people would keep it just as it was, with Michael to work around the place a little. Then everything would be the same, almost.

He climbed the stairs of the carriage house in excitement, for he had never been inside a carriage loft. He knocked at the door, but there was no answer. He tried again, then pounded and listened for a sound inside. Could the old man be ill or hurt, with no one to help him? He pressed the latch. The door yielded, and inside, Dirk saw quickly that Michael was not there.

In the barren room sat a canvas cot without bedding, a table, a sink, a wooden chair. A stout slingshot hung by its leather thong from a nail on one wall. A black stove was piped well out into the room. Shivering in the thick chill, Dirk opened the iron door. There was no glow inside. He felt the sides and top. Both were cold. Apparently the fire had been out for hours.

Had the red car taken Michael away? Somehow

Dirk felt sure of it. "Gypsies help gypsies," Michael had said, and "When I am old, the gypsies will come for me." And Dirk hoped they'd take him to a warmer place.

He looked at the loft doors, where hay would have been pitched up for the horses long ago. A stout stick held the hasp, but the metal looked smooth and bright. Ropes hung from the hasp. They were fastened to pegs in the floor, with ample length left over.

Feeling like an intruder, yet compelled, Dirk pulled out the stick in the hasp and unfastened the ropes. The doors swung out and he stood looking at Michael's meadow. All those paths, so open and worn that day he and Marni first came to the meadow, must have had a reason. And the sling-shot. The fleeting figure he thought he had seen that early morning could have been Michael, looking for a bit of game.

At last he fastened the doors and went downstairs. Just outside he bumped his foot. In his path lay a clod of earth, torn up by the stubborn stems and held by matted roots of meadow grass. The surface was damp to a half-inch depth. The bottom was dry. "It's for me." Said Dirk to himself. "It's fresh *patrin* and I can read it. Michael left after the storm."

A little beyond, he found a twig stuck upright in the ground, its peeled strip of bark hanging toward the road. He hurried on. But at the road he found two such twigs, the peeled strips pointing in opposite directions. Nothing more. Was Michael telling him that he himself didn't know where he was going? Or was he playing a last little joke on a *gadjo*?

Studying the two twigs, Dirk thought of Michael's words. "With the *patrin* I showed you, even police could not find the gypsies."

He smiled, feeling a little bit sad and a little bit tricked. Still, they had been friends. They had even exchanged coins. And he stood a little taller, smiling. He had had a gypsy as a friend.

13. The Meadow Measured

The first snow fell. Its wet flakes clung to one side of the great tree trunk and traced the branches windward up to their needle-slim twigs.

The shiny stream froze like a trickle of thin blue milk, and all of the meadow crowd came to slide on it. The impractical ones brought their ice skates. But it was sleds that worked best. The Lookout made a small firm hill for coasting.

Sitting beside Dirk on a frozen hump of earth, Han clapped his mittened hands and stamped his feet for warmth. "You know," he said, "the meadow's as good in winter as in summer?"

Dirk, watching the puffs of silver steam from his own breath, scarcely heard.

"Jarus? Why don't you answer?"

Dirk snatched at the vapor trail of Han's words. "It sure is," he said quickly. "The meadow sure is."

At last the sun grew surer. Hyacinths around the Jarus house sent up sturdy buds, tiny earth-movers breaking the tough ground, jacketed by a mere circlet of leaves against the cold. "They mean business," Mrs. Jarus said, and stooped to touch them.

In the meadow, the Club Forever wore a uniform of boots. Every pocket in the earth held melted snow, and there spring peepers shrieked, irresponsible with joy.

Dirk and Han and a dozen others stood at the brink of the Pit. Winds and melting snows of a hard winter had worn the sharp edges and filled some of the hollow. Wet leaves lay over the floor.

"It's not as deep as we had it," Han complained.

Dirk poked leaves with a long storm-pruned branch. "It's filled up some, all right. First thing we'll have to do is clear out the leaves and sharpen it up. We ought to start Saturday."

"This summer I get to go up the tree rope," Marni reminded him. "I'm a lot bigger now."

Dirk considered her size, remembering how promises could dog you. "Maybe by the *end* of the summer," he said.

Except for the small strip of sand, the banks of the stream were tantalizing mud.

✿   ✿   ✿

On Saturday morning, when the meadow crowd arrived with spades, they found two men there in high boots and close-fitting caps. One held an upright rod. The other, signalling, sighted through an instrument on a tripod.

"What are *they* doing in our meadow?" a small boy demanded.

Dirk stopped short. "That's surveyors' stuff."

"Ask them, anyhow, Dirk," Spook said. "Go on." And the others urged, "You ask."

Dirk advanced from the huddle. "Excuse me, sir," he said to the man taking notes at the sighting instrument, "would you tell us what's going on here?" And Spook, in the tone of a No Trespassing sign, shouted, "Yeah, what are *you* doing in here?"

Without disturbing his rhythms of work, the man looked straight ahead. "We're surveying."

From a safe distance Spook called out, "We don't want it surveyed."

"Sorry," said the surveyor, sounding busy but not sorry, and he went on with his work.

95

Someone quite young grew reckless with panic. "It's Dirk's meadow. He never told you to survey."

"Who's Dirk?" The man relaxed a moment and looked around.

Half a dozen of the meadow crowd shouted, "Here's Dirk," and "This is him," and "The woman that owns it—she *told* him the meadow was for us."

"She promised." From Marni it sounded legal and awesome and world-without-end.

The man took time to look from one to another of the meadow crowd. Then he spoke, not unkindly. "There'll be buildings going up here," he said.

✷   ✷   ✷

When Dirk and Han came into the farmhouse, Mr. Jarus was inspecting a doorframe torn by a loose hinge. "Marni," he called, "have you been swinging from the doorknobs again?"

"Not very much, Daddy." And Marni added, "You did say this house is stronger than a new one."

"Well, you can stop it. Dirk, bring me that tube of wood filler from the wagonshed, will you?" He was still glowering at the doorframe when Dirk came back, and only when he finished his chore did he really look at Han and Dirk. "What's up?"

"They're surveying the meadow," said both boys at once.

Mr. Jarus slowly replaced the cap on the tube. "Well, then it's happened."

"What's happened?" said Dirk. Something was coming to an end. You knew it with a leaden kind of knowing. And still you hoped.

Mr. Jarus whipped a small chair around and sat across it with his arms on the back. "When the woman in the stone house died," he began, "she was at the end of an old-fashioned fortune and deep in bank mortgages. Now someone has bought the meadow and seems to have plans for it."

"Plans," said Dirk. "Why couldn't all of us have bought the meadow? All together we might have bought it."

"We did think of that. Some of us talked about it. But it didn't work out. So then we hoped someone would buy the house and meadow together and leave it as it was, the way the woman in the stone house did. She told you she would, and she did. It looks as if the next owner won't."

"I never thought about it like that," said Han. "She must have *liked* kids."

14. A Kind Of Night

It is a delicate day. The long snows have re-
freshed the earth, and it is green. The giant tree
has blossomed and its seeds have ripened and
fallen, a few to take root as they have for more
than a hundred years. An oriole's nest swings again
from the end of a branch. This is the day the
machinery comes.

It comes with a rumble, early. Children run out
to see. "Lookit the big Cat," shouts one who has
learned his vehicles. "A parade," another rejoices.
They are very young.

First the bulldozer rolls in on massive treads. Behind it is the backhoe, with cupped metal hand and
stub fingers. A heavy open truck catches up with
them.

Two handsome cars have just been parked at the road. The men who get out of them are dressed in striped sports jackets. They walk like men accustomed to directing.

In the meadow, little knots of best friends gather. Way back that cold Saturday, the surveyors had said it would happen, and after that, the meadow crowd had talked about it a little. But now it had been a long time and nothing had changed. So, because it hadn't changed, the change might never come.

The bulldozer and the backhoe roll ahead, leaving broad tracks in the meadow grass. And then they are hailed to a stop. The men in striped coats approach to confer. They look in this direction and that, pointing. They consult a paper plan and shake their heads. Something seems to be wrong.

A mistake! A stir passes from one group of watchers to another. They'd got the wrong street. It happened all the time here with taxis and delivery trucks, ever since somebody carried off the street signs last Halloween.

But the delay is short. The vehicles roll on and veer toward the cut woodland, the children walking after, slowly.

Now the wheels and caterpillar treads are in position, and the work and the sound of work begin. The stub fingers of the backhoe grope around Marni's tree-stump table. The cupped hand sinks deep, deeper. It comes up with the stump, holding with care, dropping its burden with precision onto the truck. The other stumps follow.

Meanwhile the bulldozer, its blade set low, has fitted itself into the abandoned lane. Swiftly it rams the chimney wall, scattering the fieldstones and bricks. Next it treads out to the low trees. One by one the flowering hawthorns yield. They go easily, with no inconvenience to the machine.

Dirk looks up at the last choice tangle—the young buckeye that gave its rich crop for pocket trading last fall; the wild cherry, its sweet-sour fruit shared last summer by the meadow crowd and the birds; the ancient hollow apple tree he'd found for Marni's cupboard.

The three trees fall neatly and without commotion. The apple is rotted inside. A strong wind could have taken it down.

Goodbye, Run Sheep Run, goodbye. Goodbye, moonlit nights and the secret airborne signals; the running, swift and soundless and out of sight before fresh signals warn, "The enemy is close!" when parents' curfew soon will sound; when loss of game is loss of very self. Goodbye then, all that dear desperation. There are no more hiding places now.

No more hiding places? That is not quite true. To be sure, familiar things are gone. The meadow is almost levelled. But well toward the edge of it and almost apart, like a mountain built into the landscape, there remains the one soaring tree.

It is to the tree that Han looks now, then back to the machinery. "They won't," he begins to say, but his words are stuck.

Dirk shifts his weight. "Tree's too big. You know what that tree is. It's got a trunk like granite."

Rocco has overheard. "Too big, huh? Listen, you know what a bulldozer can do? A bulldozer can do anything, my father says."

"So what if it can," says Dirk. "The tree's way out at the edge. They'd be stupid to take it. Plain stupid. They can build their buildings this side of it."

"Stupid, huh?" says Rocco. "They got to clear a site. What do you think they do with a bulldozer? Do you think they say, 'Oh, push this over, oh, leave that'? Hah, they take it all, boy. They do these things big."

The younger children study Rocco now to know

what to believe. Rocco's father owns a cement mixer. Rocco even knew the words. *Clear a site.* But Rocco isn't the leader of the meadow crowd. He tries to be, but he isn't.

"Tree's too big," Dirk had said. They'd heard him. And they know their tree.

But even now, the bulldozer is rolling toward it.

Marni, standing in a little frozen group, sees the machine's direction. She breaks from the rest and runs to the tree. Four young children follow. For a second they stand, without a word, without a plan. Then with a single motion, they join hands, their eyes still toward the bulldozer. They are a defiant circle now, their backs to the colossus of the trunk.

The dogs catch urgency from the children. They rush in with Pancho in the lead, squatting on their forequarters to menace the machine with ridiculous growls and yelps.

Till now the presence of the children has been allowed. They have been well-behaved and quiet, and willing to watch from a distance. The men in charge are used to spectators, and what they have to do today is something special. Never before have they cleared a building site with a tree so big. The stripes of their coats say it is an occasion.

102

But here is interference. These children are not applauding. They are excited and hostile. Someone could get hurt around this machinery and cause a lawsuit.

The man in red stripes advances. "Get those kids out of here." He waves his arm for them to go away. Parents have been watching from the windows. Now they, too, come out to the meadow, and call the children in.

✿   ✿   ✿

When all the children are cleared away, the bulldozer sets about its work, quivering a little. Then it comes on, stopping just short of the trunk. There the blade is raised high, slanting against the heavy lowest branch for leverage.

The bulldozer backs up and, pausing to shift gears, it comes on with a thrust. It backs away again. This time it tries from another angle, for the tree is free to fall in any direction except toward the creek. And the crawler treads come on again.

But this is only testing, busywork till the time comes to perform. The work now is for the other machine and, as the striped coats confer, the backhoe wheels into position.

At a short distance out from the trunk, the mechanical arm.is mechanically raised and the stub-fingered hand is forced down to chop the earth. There is a sound of cracking roots. Inside the house, Marni covers her ears.

The backhoe moves slightly to the right. Again the hand is raised and again it comes down with force. So, continuing around the tree, a trench is dug. The digging is tidy. Only a dainty sprinkling of earth borders it. Now, with its root base narrowed, the tree is considered ready for the next stage.

It must have been assumed that a tree so big, so old, might well be hollow inside and would give way easily. The bulldozer is ready and confident. It has rehearsed. It snorts, rattles, and takes its bearings. And then it comes on with a charge.

The impact is harsh. The man in the seat is severely shaken. But the great monolith of trunk casts off the machine. It needs no weapon in return. It needs only to stand, and not the tremor of a leaf will say that the blow is felt.

The driver shifts gears, the crawler backs away. It pauses for another shift, and then it comes on again. Charge. Charge. And charge.

The bulldozer manoeuvers nervously. It works its way backward. Across the meadow, Pancho howls.

Now the machine pauses to come on again, its raised blade like an ancient shield for hand-to-hand combat against a mighty foe. Charge. Charge. And charge. Pale nicks begin to show in the bark. They are surface scratches. No more than that.

Again the bulldozer moves back. And again it comes on. Charge. Charge. And charge. But the tree will not give up. Though its roots are cut in a trench all round, a thousand furious toes still grip the earth.

The men in striped coats blot their faces with fresh white handkerchiefs and confer again. "Stand by," the man in red stripes calls toward the bull-dozer. Then he walks to the tree's dripline and ges-tures. It is evident that he is speaking of the tree's balance—so much for height and spread, so much for the root base.

Another trench will be dug, farther from the trunk and deeper.

It is the backhoe's turn again. This time the hand scoops so deeply it is lost to sight from the watch-ers at the windows. Again there is the sound of cracking roots. Earth from the digging mounts in a second circle around the tree. The circle is larger, the mound higher.

Another day, another reason for the digging, the clotted clay would have made ideal earthworks for an imaginary battle. But now all the children have gone from the meadow. Hours ago the parents called them in. It is a kind of night.

15. A Balance Shifted

Inside the Jarus house Marni and Linda, Dirk and Han have been watching, almost silent.

Marni clenches her fists against her cheeks. "Why doesn't a judge come and make them stop?"

Her mother, trimming the crust for blueberry pie, looks out the window. Two lines mark her usually calm forehead. Otherwise she appears as usual. "They are not breaking a law, Marni."

"What about the law inside of us? Daddy said there's a law inside of us."

Her mother revolves the pie plate expertly on the finger tips of one hand. She presses the crust edge with the tines of a fork.

Mr. Jarus, in a voice like someone else's, says, "There are more and more people in the world, so there have to be more and more places where they can live."

"There are other places," says Marni. "Places that don't matter. Why did they have to come here and take our meadow and our tree?"

"They were able to buy the meadow for a low price to make a better investment."

"What's an investment?"

"A way to make money earn more money."

"I hate money."

"That's silly, Marni." Linda, standing cool and proper as a child fashion model, studies Marni with the crunched shirt and jeans, hair worried into tangles, streaked face. And when Marni shows no conscience about this condition, she adds, "You're not supposed to show your feelings, Marni. It's very rude."

"I don't care."

"Oh, Marni, it's just a tree-ee."

Marni turns on her. "You don't care what happens to our meadow and our tree?"

Linda lifts her shoulders. "My mother says we won't be here long."

When Linda tires of watching and has gone home, Marni flings herself at her father's chair.

"Did I make it happen with my gypsy curse?"

Mr. Jarus lifts a tangle of her hair. "No, Marni," he says. "It wasn't you."

✿   ✿   ✿

For nearly four hours the man on the bulldozer has been working. His blue shirt is dark with patches of sweat. Flying earth has stained the trim striped coats. One of the men shakes his head.

"Should have waited till we could get the other 'dozer."

His partner answers, "It's a tougher one than I thought."

Lunge, retreat. Lunge, retreat. Lunge. And lunge. And lunge. The man behind the blade tenses himself for every blow. He looks ill, as if he might fall from the machine.

Lunge. Retreat. Lunge. Retreat. Lunge. And lunge. And lunge.

And then something more begins to happen. The watchers indoors see it. High in the air, the outermost leaves begin to tremble. The balance of strength is shifting. From the striped coats, a cheer goes up.

After the first trembling of leaves, it is only an-

110

other hour. More and more the outermost twigs shudder. Less and less does the tree resist. The oriole's nest swings from its handles.

At last the moment comes. There is a sound of sucking and gasping, of cracking and tearing. Slowly the tree tips to one side, carrying up a great clot of wounded roots.

For a long second it hesitates in mid-air. And then it falls.

The men in striped coats stand still, looking in what seems to be surprise at the abrupt emptiness of sky above the fallen tree. In a moment they recover. They have a word with the man on the bulldozer and they look at their wrist watches. The backhoe has already gone, assured that its work is done.

Then the men in charge leave. They walk with confidence, as when they came here hours ago, and they talk with vivid nods. Their gestures live over the problems of the project all the way to the street. There they part to get into their cars at once. And they drive away in a burst of noise and speed, for they have worked far into their Saturday afternoon, which should have been free.

16. The Little Facts And The Big Fact

On Sunday no machinery came. The tree lay on the ground, but its twigs were so full of juices that the young leaves stayed crisp, as if the tree still grew.

The meadow crowd gathered early. Yesterday they had all seen the machinery close at hand. They had seen their chimney wall fly into bits and the buckeye tree and the apple and the hawthorns go down. And, from their windows after hours of watching, they had seen the big tree fall. When you saw something happen stroke by stroke and heard it there before you, it had to be so.

And still they returned to the meadow. Perhaps the smallest ones had thought they might wake up on Sunday to see the big tree somehow standing again, the hawthorns rooted and real, a goldfinch streaking low to camouflage his feathers against the early sunbeams, a young rabbit freezing, pretending not to be there, when all the while they could see the fur trembling over his wild heart.

Since they had seen the meadow go, night had come. And night was magic. Hadn't Dirk told them, "At night the hawthorns grow bigger and creep toward you?" Hadn't the smallest of them, about to go alone into night in a dark room, heard a departing grownup say, "Everything is all right. Tomorrow will be a fine day"? And tomorrow would be a fine day.

For the older ones, it was different. "There's the fact," Dirk said.

Whether you looked at it or away from it, he said, there you saw it just the same where the meadow had been, because it was a fact. There were little facts like you're thirsty or four hot dogs can make you sick at your stomach, or even, you got a bad mark on your report card. And there were big facts like—Dirk stopped. Every day you could read about big facts and hear about them—wars and earthquakes and traffic crashes. But, though some of their fathers had been in a war, nothing like those

113

big facts had ever happened to the meadow crowd.

"Big facts like what?" Spook said.

And with nothing after all to compare, Dirk answered, "Like the fact that we don't have the meadow now."

With the little facts, nothing much was changed for very long, but with a big fact you went back to have another look.

And so they returned to the meadow. They came without plan, and they all got there at about the same time. That was not strange. The digging of the Pit had started each day at dawn. After that, early rising had been easy, for each morning in the meadow had been a first one, really. Each morning the meadow had looked freshly thought up, and just for them.

So now in the morning, they stood at the big tree. Han knelt at the trunk. "There's our old gypsy harness hook. Underneath. See?" He spoke as if some one were asking.

Dirk began to disentangle a bit of the rope they'd knotted for climbing, but the rope, like the harness hook, had become a part of the tree, blended with it by sun and rain. In the end he let it be.

Marni stooped to cup the oriole's nest in one

114

hand. It had been built well. The basket handle still gripped the twig. "Looks like it was four eggs," said Spook.

Rocco found a shattered shell thrown well clear of the tree. "You thought that old bulldozer couldn't do it?" But then he turned to the shell and said, "Looks like writing on it. What do you know? Like writing."

Linda came up behind Marni, arriving a little later than the rest. "Come on, Marni. I've got these old clothes on. We can sit on the branches and bounce."

Marni turned slowly. "Why don't you go home, Linda? Just go home." And she found a terrible comfort in being rude.

The next day a truck came in with a power saw, and a keening sound rose and fell, hill after hill of it, and over and under it, a sound of purpose, a sound of sharpness over toughness, a sound of persistence that would win.

Trunk and roots and branches were cut into convenient sizes to haul away. The gap in the earth where the roots had grown was filled in. So, too, were the holes left by the patch of tree stumps. So, too, was the Pit, leveled with the Lookout.

In the next days the shiny stream disappeared, captured in tiles and covered with earth, and so it was a ghost curve now that the line of houses followed. Only the dip of terrain stayed to tell the stream's course.

The scrap of road past the burned tenant house was declared a street. Another street would take most of the field between the stone house and the Jarus place. Construction gear rolled in to begin building apartments on the meadow site, and on nearby vacant lots, new frames went up.

Now the only patch of wildness was inside the hedge of the stone house. In the absence of Michael, tangles sprang up, and the place grew more and more alluring to the meadow crowd. "It should ought to be haunted," said Spook, hopefully.

But something was wrong. "Whatsa matter, Dirk? Why don't you ever stay?" Rocco complained as he and Spook and Han followed Dirk home.

Dirk sat on his back doorstep. "I don't know. I feel kind of mean, running around that house yelling."

"What kind of a reason is that?" Rocco demanded. "Everybody's waiting for you out there. That's what ought to make you feel mean."

117

And, "For Pete's sake, why?" Spook said. "Nobody lives there. Nobody cares. We're not hurting anything."

It was hard to put into words, and even if he could, Dirk guessed he wouldn't want to, even to Han. It had something to do with the old lady saying, "You will come back, won't you?" And the way he'd managed not to.

But that had nothing to do with the others. "Go on back," he urged them. "Maybe I'll come over later. I told my Dad I'd help him move some stuff upstairs. It's heavy stuff."

Days went by, and Dirk still avoided the stone house. And without him, it wasn't the same for the others.

Not far away, a shopping center was being finished, and the stores drew them all for a time, to spend their pocket money, or just to watch for new items of stock. But Dirk and the older boys soon tired of that, and even the younger ones began to drift away.

"There's nothing to do," the meadow crowd said.

✳   ✳   ✳

"Nothing to do? What's all this about? Everyone

I know has trouble finding time enough. Here, you can give me a hand with these dishes." And Mrs. Jarus tied a red-checked apron around Dirk and gave Marni a tea towel to match it, lifting a smooth pile of towels to find the right one.

Marni, feeling somehow ambushed, dried plates in silence.

Dirk submerged a muffin pan in suds. His mother was so darn cheerful, tying an apron on him, giving him a push into a job that sat right there before him. "Oh, sure," he said, "there's something to do. That's not what I meant."

"That's what you said. But you have friends and parties and a good school and nice vacations. You have music lessons, and a concert now and then, and a good library, and books of your own. And you have movies and TV. You don't seem to realize it, but you're very fortunate."

Dirk scratched at a charred raisin that stuck to the pan. She sounded as if she'd just baked a thousand cookies for the PTA, and now people were eating them as if they were only store cookies.

"And what about the places we show you? Just last week, for instance, we drove a hundred miles to take you to a good aquarium."

"I'd rather catch one crawdad at the creek," said Marni ungratefully.

Mrs. Jarus made an exasperated sound. "What is it you two want—this side of the moon?"

And Dirk said, "Oh, we can keep busy, if you mean doing *anything,* just so we're doing *something.* All that stuff they think up for kids is O.K. It's supposed to keep us out of trouble, I guess. But sometimes you like it when nothing is figured out for you." He found he couldn't say it without saying it. "Like in the meadow. The meadow was just there and we thought up our own things to do in it."

"But the meadow is gone. Now isn't it time you faced up to what's happened and got back to normal? Nothing you can do will bring the meadow and the big tree back. They—won't—be—back."

A level clank of dishes was the only response. Back to normal? What was normal now? Everything was all mixed up.

"Actually," said Mrs. Jarus briskly, "You should be thinking you were lucky that you had the meadow at all. There aren't many places like that these days. So why don't you two put the whole thing out of your minds and stop moping?"

Moping. It was a word Marni had heard before when she hadn't had time to feel out her feelings. When bad things happened to grownups, were they able to put the whole thing out of their minds?

Dirk found words for her. "Nobody's moping, Mom. Nobody's going to crack up about it."

"Good. Now, have you been out there to see what they're doing, how they put up these buildings —the excavations and the footings, the steel girders and the concrete floorings? I'd think you'd be out there watching."

And then Marni found her voice. "We wouldn't go near any of that. Nobody in our whole Club Forever would. Little kids might. Little kids that think it's great just to see any old truck go by. But not us older ones. Not any of the meadow crowd. We're staying away."

Dirk bumped a heap of bluish powder into the sink and scoured mightily. Marni dried the last dish, and Mrs. Jarus put it away on a high shelf. Then Dirk said patiently, "Can I go now?"

Mrs. Jarus looked at Marni, then at Dirk. "Go ahead."

17. Another Find

Dirk, Han, Spook, and Rocco poked around in the Jarus wagonshed. Dirk looked at the overstocked floor and shelves, feeling somehow the visitor now. For the first time, he saw what his mother meant about the wagonshed. For the first time, he saw the place unkempt, with an earth floor and a mousy smell, and filled with snips and bits that nobody else much would even keep. Today, the inside of the wagonshed was just a junk heap.

And in a little panic, he thought maybe that's how you felt about places like this when you were grown up. All the good messy stuff that sat around inviting you when you were a kid—maybe it stopped saying anything to you.

He'd test that theory out. There was the lumber

pile still sitting, waiting. There were the ladders and the coils of rope and wire, the paint, the glue, the litter of tools and leftover materials, just as before. He looked into a tray of trivia, and he was uninspired.

✿   ✿   ✿

"Funny thing," he said. "You used to look at this stuff and think of things to do with it."

He didn't like the way he felt. It was like having no feeling at all. "Let's get out of here," he said.

Outside, the wagonshed was O.K., even for grown-ups. It wasn't just walls and windows. It was neat and white, and it kind of talked to you, like the house.

Rocco, at the fence, choosily picked off a brown and yellow honeysuckle horn and ate it. "What's to do today?"

Dirk glared at the newly finished buildings set on the meadow, the meadow cleared now of stump and fieldstone, upholstered with intentional grass and pronounced a playground. "Nothing, I guess."

Between the two nearest buildings he could see across the playground and between two others beyond. "Anyhow, Porter, I can still see part of your house. We can still fly signals." They hadn't flown signals for a long time, and all at once, he knew that flying signals was kid stuff.

It seemed ages since there had been a meadow. He felt different now, the way an older person is different. He thought of how his grandfather used to reach for his pipe, give his chair a little hitch, and begin, "In my experience—"

At first, experience had been just the sound of a word, smooth and polished as a little carving you'd want to hold in your hand. Then after a while, experience was something that happened to others, but it was always a far-off thing. It was for people with bushy white eyebrows and a certain chair with deep hollows in the cushions.

But now, experience had come to you, too. You saw your meadow go. All in one day it went, with a tree that took more than a hundred years to get that big. It went. What came to you instead was experience. And you began to be old.

Spook pointed across the playground. "There's a van turning in. Somebody's starting to move into these darned buildings. Well, I'm not going to like anybody there. Not if he's the King of Siam, I won't."

"Me, neither," Han pledged.

What had happened to the meadow was happening everywhere, they kept telling you. So what were you supposed to do? Stand there and say, "Great. Look at progress"? Dirk struck a furious fist on the fence. "They could have left something. There was room. They could have left the big tree and still built as many stupid buildings. They could have left some *little trees*. Why didn't they *leave* something?"

"They could have," Han said.

"You'd think," said Dirk, "if they wanted a desert so bad, they'd go where there was one already. But no. They had to go and make a new one. Well, they got one. With a bulldozer it's easy. Anybody could do it. Marni could. What's so great about that?"

"Marni could," said Han, "but she wouldn't. None of us would."

This feeling of being older, Dirk thought—even before the meadow went, he'd had that. A long time ago he'd rushed from breakfast out to the thicket, and after that, a lot of things were changed. And he said, "Did I ever tell you about the thicket?"

"No."

"Right where all your houses are, there was a

126

big old wild grapevine you could swing on. We had an owl and a raccoon there."

Han, chewing on a sprig of mint from Mrs. Jarus' kitchen garden, gulped. "Gee, we were the ones that really wrecked your thicket. It was our houses wrecked it."

"You didn't, either." But then Dirk remembered how that other Dirk, way back, had felt. "Sure, the thicket got mashed, but it wasn't your fault. We had our best times after you and Spook and Rocco and the rest moved here. You ought to know that much, Porter. You ought to know that, you guys."

The thicket was one thing, and it had sort of settled itself. But with the meadow, it couldn't work the same way. Too much was different.

Han spoiled some of the perfect grass with the edge of his shoe and growled, "We did have good times."

Now Han was talking old, too, like parents telling how they cracked hickory nuts and had a country kind of fun, saying something was all over.

Why couldn't anything ever stay the way it was? Why did everything always have to get torn up? You kept having to make a choice, and that was hard to do. But when a bulldozer mashed up the meadow and knocked down the big tree, you had no choice at all. And that was harder.

Dirk turned away and pretended to look for a certain size of mint leaf. Stooping, he could smell the cool mint growing in the cool earth. It was nice here in the shade. You didn't feel so mad and so mixed up. And as always, he examined the ground, indebted as he was to it for luck.

Once again, he found something. It was a low twiggy thing, and he called out, "Hey-y, this is no mint. This has a hard stem." He felt the rough leaves. "What do you know? It's a little elm tree sprouted."

"Off our big tree?" The others crouched around.

"Sure. It has to be. Listen, we got to make a fence around that." He shot an accusing look toward the farmhouse kitchen. "Somebody'll think it's a weed and jerk it out."

In the wagonshed they found strips of wood. Dirk shook a paint can with dried dribbles of blue, listening for the thick slurp of vital signs. Old brushes were soaking in coffee cans for just such an emergency.

"The way you got to do it," Rocco said, "you

128

paint the sticks, and tomorrow when they're dry, you make the fence."

Dirk frowned. "By tomorrow a cat could walk on that tree and bust it off."

Han, carrying sticks out of the wagonshed, looked back at the doorway. "There's a lot of swell junk in there," he sighed.

When their work was done, they stood over the blue-dribbled mint to admire. Dirk looked across the new playground, shutting out everything but what he remembered there. "Gee, for one little seed, that came a long way."

But from the entrance of the actual masonry there, a boy came out. He was about Dirk's and Han's age, his clothes agreeably sloppy, his head alert. Even from this distance, they could see he was scouting.

"Look's as if that guy's going to live there," said Spook, with sudden hospitality.

"It does, at that," Han agreed.

Dirk blinked. "What's the matter with me," he said to himself, "still seeing the meadow out there? The meadow is gone, as Mom said."

And still he felt an odd sort of restlessness, as if that seen and known fact didn't quite settle it.

18. Toward Meadow Tangles

"A meadow? A tree that big? A little creek?"

The questions rose inside the Jarus wagonshed, where new young people numbered as many as the old meadow crowd. Probably no one there could have said just why they had gathered, but the newcomers had been pronounced O.K. and, as in the days of the Pit and the Lookout, everyone close by had drifted over.

Boys hung from shelves, relaxed as pendant possums. Others sat on upturned crates or minnow pails or the woodpile. Overhead, loops of cobwebs swayed richly, weighted with dust, and from the floor came the haunting smell of earth.

"When was all that?" someone asked.

Marni hunched forward, chin in hands, eyes filled

with a private vision of the past, a summer ago. "Once."

Dirk teetered on an upsided seedling flat. Everyone there had heard about the meadow now, in a sort of initiation. But why would the new people give a hoot?

If you'd never slipped past your pursuers in the conspiracy of code and summer dusk, or lain listening to the crickety grass at night, watching the trees creep toward you, or seen gypsy wagons plainer than real ones could be; if you'd never dug a Pit in summer sun or found nests of small wild animals, or felt the tingle at the top of your head when you sat in the big tree, or even wished yourself up in it when you'd be older, how could you care?

Then Dave, the boy he'd seen that day from the mint bed, said, "At the stone house there's wild stuff. I saw inside the hedge."

"But you can't go in there for fun anymore," Spook advised him.

"Why not?"

"Because it's a museum now. You have to keep out."

A younger new boy, Pinky, scratched the earth

131

floor with a stick. "I had a good place once. Way behind my house I had a tree. And all around the bottom of the tree there was this bush—had long stems on it that rolled under and made a tunnel. You could crawl through that tunnel and sit behind the leaves. On an old rock."

Spook, beginning to tie a raveled shoe lace, let it go. "Why'd you move away from *that*?"

"Aw, my father got this better job. But I don't care. They wrecked my bush and spoiled my tunnel."

Spook turned the bruise-blue of his eyes on Pinky. "Wouldn't they even leave you have a *tunnel*?"

"Huh-uh. The bush was messy, they said. Too wild. They dug it up." He gouged a harsh zigzag and drove the point of his stick into the floor. *I'll never tell them I had a tunnel in it.*"

The comradely silence was broken by Han. "Messy—around houses everything is too *prissy*. What good is outdoors anymore? Just grass to keep off of."

"And geran-i-ums," said Spook with loathing. "No wonder the gypsies went, even Michael. The gypsies got dis-gusted, everything so purr-fict."

"Perfect, that's the way they want it," said Han.

132

A low roll, a sound of distant revolution, of possible attack at dawn, swept the wagonshed. "They!" and "So purr-fict." And it came to a frustrated end.

"They" decided. That was the thing. Now Dirk understood why his father wanted the wagonshed saved. Maybe "they," the rest of them, had only forgotten what it was like to be a kid. The meadow was gone, all right, but maybe there *was* something you could do about it, something you could settle for. Even now the big tree was making a fresh start in the mint bed, with a painted fence around it to say, "This is important."

And he called out to the others, "Why don't we get some wild stuff and build tangles back again, the way they were in the meadow?"

"Get wild stuff back?"

"Sure, everything in the meadow was always loaded with seeds. There must be plenty of good stuff coming up right now. We could dig it up and put it together and make our own tangles."

Pinky, grown attached to his misery, moped along with Spook. "If there's a lot of good stuff coming up, then why is there just grass and ger-an-i-ums?"

"Because they keep tearing the wild stuff out,"

133

said Dirk. "But if we went around and got to it first—"

Han appeared to see a fast-run film of burgeoning branches plunge upward through the roof. "We could grow whole *forests*."

"Where?" said a mocking voice, Rocco's.

"Well, most everybody here has *some* ground," Dirk said. "And where people's grass joins in the back, the *tangles* could join." He thought of the dusty play yards he'd seen near the tracks on his first day in town, and a fullblown picture came to him. "Say, in a whole block of houses, everybody could walk out his own back door into a little meadow."

"What about us?" said Dave, and added, "You'd think with all the silly playground grass out there just sitting, they'd let go of a little piece."

Rocco still stayed aloof. "Before we grew tangles that were any good, we'd all be a hundred years old."

"A hundred!" said Dirk. "Look at what came up at the stone house in just one summer, with Michael gone. Listen, there's a vine that's supposed to grow so fast, it's practically an instant tangle. The thing we got to remember is: Stuff *wants* to grow."

134

Here Spook, with his odd gift, rose into the air in a way to blur the boundaries of the possible, and on his way to ordinary earth again, he rejoiced, "Rabbits would come back. Raccoons, too, I bet."

The consensus came. "Yay-y-y!"

This was the beginning. The younger ones had a parade. "They," who grew the perfect grass and geraniums, and nothing else, were not all as formidable as they had been pictured. Many did have stray growth for new meadow spots. Some had chores to offer, and the earned money bought shrubs and little trees that gave the plan a hurried boost. Some of them hired landscapers to make their tangles look just right.

The wagonshed became the report center for the young crowd.

All that fall, Dirk, Han, and Dave worked hard with the rest, discovering, digging up—an elderberry shoot, a lilac, a thorn tree, a raspberry cane —reminders of the meadow, to build new wild spots. The sprout from the giant elm tree prospered.

Soaked by snow and rain, sunned and blown, new growth shot out by spring. The word traveled. The school paper and the local paper carried it. Eventually, the big city paper nearby and a much-read magazine would print stories about the meadow crowd's work.

For Dirk, Han, and Dave, there was little free time left. But Dirk felt ready now to fold up those earlier years and put them away. "I guess the younger ones will have to operate the tangles now," he told Marni.

The younger ones did operate the tangles. Among them all, only Linda lost interest. She left the meadow crowd early, to be with older girls.

Home for spring holidays a few years later, Dirk walked into town with Han and Dave. On Main Street they bought hot buttered popcorn to share from one large sack—one sack for three boys. You weren't so public about your hunger now.

Dirk looked down the hill toward the seedy area by the freight tracks. And with a touch of the new grandness of being away at school, he said, "Let's see what the rest of the old town looks like."

The houses were still unpainted and surely a little shabbier. But paint seemed of less consequence now, for clumps of greenness had sprung up all around.

"Did we do that, too?" said Han.

One sizeable tree stood out from the haze of

shrubs, and from an obliging branch, a boy swung out.

"Like our old grapevine swing!" said Dirk, and he added, "Way down here." He remembered these houses from that first day in town, and he remembered his quick and formless sadness for them then. "Way down here," he said again. "Maybe this is where they need some tangles most of all."

Dave looked puzzled. "What did you say?"

But Dirk had stopped. "Listen," he said, and they all did.

There was singing. The excited peepers trilled as if in country puddles, and a flurry of birds shopped the growing wildness.

And so in time, this small city has become rather famous because of a boy named Dirk and because of his friends. Once they had a meadow with low hawthorns and a tiny stream and a giant tree. They had that meadow for a summer and a winter, and they had it just as if it were their own.

Now wild patches flourish there, refreshing the whole city; and the children, the small woods creatures, and even "they" like it that way.

The first rabbit appeared long ago. Spook reported it. Soon the young oaks will be old enough to bear acorns, and when that time comes, the squirrels, blue jays and chipmunks will know.

No owls have come yet, but Marni watches for them and listens. "A hollow tree might help," she says. "But that takes longer. It takes a long time," says Marni, "to grow a hollow tree."

About the Author and Artist

Ethel Collier's previous books for children — *I Know A Farm, The Birthday Tree,* and *Who Goes There In My Garden?*—were written within the limits of a vocabulary especially chosen to help readers who, for the first time, are reading. The imaginativeness of her response to that restrictive situation produced books that were not only *not* a chore—but, more importantly, not a bore. The same challenging perceptiveness goes into *The Gypsy Tree,* a book in more extended form and for older interests.

Mrs. Collier is an active member of the Author's League, "seeking more members for more dues for better copyright laws." Her interests and her training at the University of Michigan were all focused toward writing, and she not only plunged into journalism but married a journalist. Her home in Cleveland, Ohio, was in her mind's eye as she wrote this story.

To the eyes of Lajos Szalay, the American scene is recent, so that, though his work has been published and revered in Budapest, Tucumán (Argentina), Buenos Aires, and Munich, this is the first book he has illustrated in the United States, his home since 1960.

Perhaps the intensity with which he sees his new land is intensified by exile from his old (Hungary), by the persecution that caused it, and by the periods of privation inevitable to it.